GREG the SAUSAGE ROLL

Egg-cellent Easter Adventure

To Phoenix and Kobe, never give up on your dreams.
Love Mum and Dad xx - R. H. and M. H.

For Paul, Julia and Tracey, from your
EGGcellent brother (brother-in-law). - G. C.

PUFFIN BOOKS

UK | USA | Canada | Ireland | Australia | India | New Zealand | South Africa

Puffin Books is part of the Penguin Random House group of companies whose addresses can be found at global.penguinrandomhouse.com

www.penguin.co.uk   www.puffin.co.uk   www.ladybird.co.uk

 Penguin
Random House
UK

First published 2024

001

Text and illustrations copyright © Mark and Roxanne Hoyle, 2024
Illustrations by Gareth Conway

The moral right of the authors has been asserted.

Printed and bound in Italy

The authorized representative in the EEA is Penguin Random House Ireland, Morrison Chambers, 32 Nassau Street, Dublin D02 YH68

A CIP catalogue record for this book is available from the British Library

ISBN: 978-0-241-63112-6

All correspondence to: Puffin Books, Penguin Random House Children's, One Embassy Gardens, 8 Viaduct Gardens, London SW11 7BW

FSC
www.fsc.org
MIX
Paper | Supporting
responsible forestry
FSC® C018179

GREG the SAUSAGE ROLL

Egg-cellent Easter Adventure

MARK AND ROXANNE HOYLE

Illustrated by Gareth Conway

PUFFIN

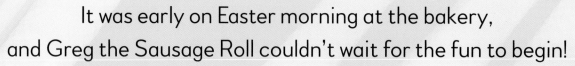

It was early on Easter morning at the bakery,
and Greg the Sausage Roll couldn't wait for the fun to begin!

Holly the baker had been busy making
chocolate nests all week, and soon
the delicious Easter eggs would be
delivered to fill them.

Greg could see Holly outside,
chatting to the delivery driver, Dave.

Greg leapt down from the window to tell Gloria what he had heard. "Something's happened to the Easter Bunny, Gloria. *I just know it.*"

"What's wrong? Take a deep breath and tell me everything," said Gloria calmly.

"If the Easter Bunny doesn't visit, the children won't get their chocolate and there'll be no EGG HUNT!" cried Greg in a panic.

"Oh, that's terrible – Easter will be ruined!" said Gloria. "But what can we do, Greg? We don't even know where she lives."

Later that morning, a little voice chirped up from below . . .

BISCUITS

NEST CAKES

"*Psssssssst* . . . We can help you!" said Lil Chick.
"We know where she lives!"

"YES, MATE!" cried Greg.
Lil Chick hopped, skipped and jumped up to the counter,
then told Greg and Gloria to listen up.

Go out of the bakery
and turn left . . .

. . . on to a GINORMOUS twirling, swirling slide!

They landed with a bump on soft green grass and looked up.

"WOW, GLORIA!" said Greg. "This is amazing!"

"I know, Greg," Gloria agreed. "It's eggs-traordinary!"

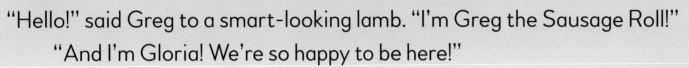

"Hello!" said Greg to a smart-looking lamb. "I'm Greg the Sausage Roll!"

"And I'm Gloria! We're so happy to be here!"

"Welcome to Easterland. I'm Gordon Lambsy," he said.
"I'd normally offer to show you around, but we've got a bit of a situation –
the Easter Bunny hasn't shown up for work!"

"I KNEW IT!" shrieked Greg. "Don't worry, Mr Lambsy – we want to help!"

"Please hurry!" said Gordon. "If we can't find her, there will be no eggs
this Easter – for ANYONE!"

"You can count on us," said Greg.
"Off we go, Gloria –
we've got a case to crack!"

But Easterland was so much fun that Greg and Gloria got a little distracted. Gloria was egg-cited to see where all the wrapping took place!

And Greg LOVED helping the chicks paint the eggs, even if he did get a bit messy.

But he had the MOST fun with the egg-maker machine!

"Glooooorrrriiiiaaaaaa!" Greg called. "Look what's happened!"

"Oh, it's a Gr-EGG! You crack me up!" said Gloria. "Come on, I'll help you out – then we *really* have to find the Easter Bunny."

But just then, Greg spotted something irresistible . . .
"Oh, Gloria, look! It's a zip wire. We have to see where it goes!"

"WHEEEEEEEEEEEEEEEEEEEEEE!"

"This way, Greg – look!"
Gloria said.

They ran down, down, down,
through another tunnel . . .

. . . into the Easter Bunny's burrow!

"Hello, Easter Bunny!" said Greg.
"I'm Greg and this is my sweetheart, Gloria.
We're so happy to meet you!"

"Hello, and welcome
to Easterland," the Easter Bunny
replied with a sigh.

Gloria was puzzled. "Are you OK?" she asked gently. "Do you feel poorly?"

The Easter Bunny looked up – and burst into tears!

Greg and Gloria rushed over to give her a big cuddle.
"What's the matter?" asked Greg.

"I've got these new glasses," the Easter Bunny wailed, "and every time I hop anywhere, they fly off my head. Then I can't see where I'm going, so I can't hide the eggs! Easter's going to be ruined for everyone!"

Greg and Gloria gave the Easter Bunny an egg-stra big squeeze.
"Don't worry about a thing. We're here to help!" said Greg.
"That's what friends are for!" smiled Gloria.
"We'll hatch a brilliant plan to save Easter – you'll see!'

"And not just us – ALL your friends in Easterland will want to help, too," beamed Greg. "We need to get everyone together straight away."

"Leave that to me!" cried the Easter Bunny, dashing to her carrot phone.
"EASTERLAND, ASSEMBLE! Be ready in FIVE!"

"GO, TEAM EASTER!"

Back up in Easterland, everyone was ready to hop to it!
"I know just what we need!" said Gloria.

"A handful of lambswool . . .

your strongest Easter
wrapping paper . . .

and your most favourite and magical Easter ribbon."

TA-DA!!!

Before she knew it, the Easter Bunny was trying on her brand-new Easter bonnet, complete with built-in specs – handmade by Greg, Gloria and everyone in Easterland!

"It's EGGS-ACTLY what I needed" The Easter Bunny beamed.

"You're the best friends I could wish for!

Now – LET'S GET CRACKING!"

Greg, Gloria and the Easter Bunny zoomed straight to the park to hide the Easter eggs for the big egg hunt.
Can YOU find all ten eggs?

ANNUAL EASTER-EGG TREASURE HUNT

"Thank you for helping
me save Easter. How
can I ever repay you?"
said the bunny.

"Ooh, I know," said Greg.
"Would you be our VIB
(Very Important Bunny)
at our Easter party tonight?
Pleeeeeease?!"

Everyone piled back to the bakery, where the Easter Bunny made sure that Greg, Gloria and the mini sausage rolls had the most egg-straordinary Easter party EVER! The Easter Bunny was so grateful for their help, she even taught them all her very special Easter party song.

BEST. EASTER. EVER!

EASTER TREATS